Clark helping out around the farm.
That boy is <u>Strong!</u>

DC COMICS
SECRET HERO SOCIETY

FORT SOLITUDE

Written by **Derek Fridolfs** | Illustrations by **Dustin Nguyen**

SCHOLASTIC INC.

To my sixth-grade teacher, Mr. Painter, whose imposing John Wayne–like demeanor gave way to a wry sense of humor and jokes that made my camp experience one I'll always remember.
— Derek

Always thankful to my kids, Bradley and Kaeli, for filling my days with their wonder and whimsy to fuel my imagination and for understanding from day one why their dad is always drawing. Big thank-you to my wife, Nicole, for taking care of everything around us so that I can draw so much.
— Dustin

ISBN 978-1-338-16384-1

10 9 8 7 6 5 4 3 2 1   17 18 19 20 21

PRINTED IN THE U.S.A.   23
FIRST PRINTING 2017

BOOK DESIGN BY RICK DEMONICO AND CHEUNG TAI

TO: CLARK KENT
RE: ACADEMIC EXCELLENCE REWARD

CONGRATULATIONS! YOUR RECENT ACADEMIC SCORING
HAS PLACED YOU IN THE TOP OF YOUR CLASS.
THIS QUALIFIES YOU FOR A WEEK-LONG EVERGREEN
ADVENTURE CAMP! JOIN US IN THE MOUNTAINS FOR
FRIENDLY COMPETITION AND ACTIVITIES, FOSTERING
YOUR INDEPENDENT SPIRIT, AND BUILDING
FRIENDSHIPS THAT WILL LAST A LIFETIME.

RESPOND BACK TO THE EMAIL AND MORE INFORMATION
WILL BE PROVIDED.

THANK YOU FOR TAKING YOUR STUDIES SERIOUSLY
AND WE LOOK FORWARD TO SEEING YOU SOON.

EVERGREEN ADVENTURE CAMP DIRECTOR,
MILTON

6

The Kents

Chore list

- finish baling hay
- feed the horses (replace Comet's shoe)
- milk cows
- restock chicken feed
- collect eggs from the hens
- adjust tractor wheel with Pa

8

9

CABIN 1

CABIN 2

CABIN 3

CABIN 4

CABIN 5

12

13

REQUIREMENTS

- 6:00 a.m. Rise and shine! Lights out at 9:00. Don't be caught outside at night or the Scarecrow will getcha!

  Scarecrow? Who's that?

- Dress in your camp clothes, located in each cabin.

- Everyone gets kitchen duty. Schedules are posted in each cabin. Let's get cookin'!

  Cool! I can use some of Ma's recipes.

- Perform at your absolute best in all activities and athletic competitions. There will be performance evaluations.

  That's kind of weird. I thought we were just supposed to have fun?

- If you have any questions, please see your counselors.

- Be ready for an adventure!

STORAGE CLOSET — INVENTORY REPORT

* ITEMS REMOVED FROM STUDENTS UPON ENTRY TO RETREAT
* NO ELECTRONICS ALLOWED — NO EXCEPTIONS

ITEM #	DESCRIPTION	QTY	NOTES
0001	CELL PHONE; BLACK/RED, DIAMOND DESIGN	1	BELONGS TO HARLEEN QUINZEL
0002	PORTABLE VIDEO GAME CONSOLE	1 (INCLUDES RAPID RODENT BROS DISC)	BELONGS TO BARRY ALLEN
0003	TRIDENT FORK	1	OVERSIZED UTENSIL REMOVED FROM KITCHEN BY ARTHUR CURRY
0004	HAND BUZZER	13	FOUND ON JOE KERR; ROOM CHECK FOR MORE ITEMS
0005	SET OF LOCK PICKS	4	FOUND ON SELINA KYLE
0006	COMPUTER LAPTOP W/ ENCRYPTION SOFTWARE	1	BELONGS TO BRUCE WAYNE; PENDING FURTHER REVIEW
0007	ASSORTMENT — GRAPPLE GUN, NIGHT-VISION GOGGLES, TASER	1 EACH	"PERSONAL" ITEMS OF BRUCE WAYNE; INCREASE SECURITY TO STORAGE.

CLARK'S JOURNAL

It's great seeing Diana and Bruce again! And nice to take a break from chores and the animals on the farm. But I hope Streaky stays out of that tree! Because who will get him down if I'm not there? Silly cat!

Going someplace new is a lot of fun! I'm seeing more trees and mountains than I ever have back home. All we have in Smallville are cornfields, tractors, and Sally's Malt Shop. But they do make a mean double chocolate shake!

Diana seems to be enjoying camp even more than me. I think it's because she's around the sand and beach so much back where she's from. But how can anyone be bored with that? And Bruce is Bruce. I had to twist his arm to come here. But I think he's coming around. I caught him smiling when Diana joked he looked good in shorts. He totally hates shorts!

My bunkmate's name is Arthur. I think he likes the water more than land. Makes sense since he's the camp lifeguard. He warned me about a monster in the lake. Hard to tell if he's joking or not. Diana really wants me to help her push Bruce into the water. I can't tell what she wants more . . . getting Bruce wet or me in trouble for doing it. But it's all in the name of fun, so maybe it's time to let my guard down a little.

Being here also gives me a chance to continue building my scrapbook of interesting things. There's lots to see, write down, and take photos of. They've got seven kinds of pinecones in the forests around here! And lots of neat wildlife. Whoever heard of a banana slug before? It's shaped like a banana! AND IT'S YELLOW! That's crazy!! I don't want to miss a thing!

We had our first race competition! I made sure to hold back from winning. I'm really trying to blend in. Ma and Pa would be proud. I'm not sure anyone won that race though. But that's okay. Except Director Milton and his counselors didn't approve. They really want us to do our best.

MONDAY – CALL SHEET

6:00 A.M. - **Wake Up**

8:00 - **Cabin Inspection**

8:30 - **Breakfast**

9:00 - **Assembly Hall Songs**

10:00 - **Trail Hike**

12:00 P.M. - **Lunch**

1:00 - **Hike Scrapbook**

3:00 - **ACTIVITY #2** (Archery)

5:00 - **Free Time**

7:00 - **Dinner**

8:00 - **Assembly Hall**

9:00 - **Lights Out**

BEWARE THE SCARECROW

EVERGREEN BREAKFAST MENU

EGGS, BACON, SAUSAGE, TOAST, WAFFLES, PANCAKES, CEREAL
YOGURT, FRUIT, MILK, JUICE

RECOMMENDED DAILY AMOUNTS

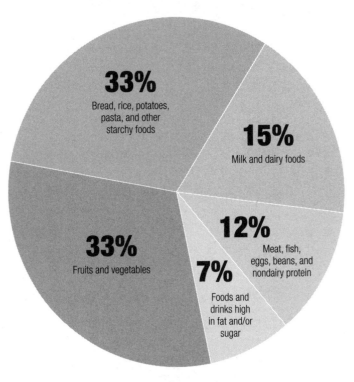

33%
Bread, rice, potatoes, pasta, and other starchy foods

15%
Milk and dairy foods

12%
Meat, fish, eggs, beans, and nondairy protein

7%
Foods and drinks high in fat and/or sugar

33%
Fruits and vegetables

* * * CALORIE COUNT, VITAMINS, AND PORTION CONTROL WILL BE MONITORED * * *

It's nice to know they want to teach good eating habits.
But this feels kind of weird. They stared at us the whole
time. It's uncomfortable to eat knowing you're being
watched. Bruce took his food into the bathroom to eat in
privacy. I really don't want to do that!!

THE EVERGREEN SONG

I am nice. I am kind.
Strong of heart and strong of mind.
Have you heard? Have you seen?
All of us at Evergreen?

Evergreeeeen, Evergreeeeen.
Always good and never mean.
Evergreeeeen, Evergreeeeen.
Come on and join our scene.

Have success. We will succeed.
Now is time to plant our seed.
We can grow, really strong.
If we all just sing along.

Evergreeeeen, Evergreeeeen.
Always good and never mean.
Evergreeeeen, Evergreeeeen.
Come on and join our scene.

25

INCIDENT REPORT

STUDENT: Barry Allen

DESCRIPTION OF THE INCIDENT:

Barry was caught putting rocks in other students'
backpacks on their hike. He acted quickly without being
seen. Many began to complain about back pain and their
bags being too heavy to carry.

ACTION TAKEN:

Barry has been given the task of sweeping out all the
cabins. When he completed the task within minutes,
he was given the additional punishment of cleaning the
latrines.

ADDITIONAL NOTES:

Barry has been described as a self-professed practical
joker. Counselors are on high alert to continue to monitor
his actions, and deal with them accordingly.

CLARK'S SCRAPBOOK

Pamela told me stay away from the poison oak. Itchy!

Kept finding these in my back-pack. That Barry is a prankster!

Found these on the hike. Ollie seems interested.

29

 It's weird not being able to text you guys. But we don't have our phones anymore.

 I'm working on that. Give me time.

 I don't mind. It's actually fun doing it this way. I pass notes all the time back in Smallville.

 That's because there's no running water or electricity in Smallville.

 Don't mind Bruce. He's mad I'm a great archer. He has lousy aim.

 I'm ignoring you both.

 I hear Floyd has left Evergreen after winning the archery contest. The counselors haven't said why.

Their excuses are as lame as yours, Clark. Which makes them suspect.

 Everyone's a suspect to Bruce.

 How are all your notes getting to me so fast?

 I've been using Barry. He offered to run like Hermes to be our messenger.

 BARRY?! That guy's trouble.

No I'm not. I'm just misunderstood.

 BARRY! This is a private conversation.

So I'm not supposed to read all these before I deliver them?

CLARK'S JOURNAL

It's our third day here and we're starting to get used to our new schedules. A lot of campers are waking up late and missing breakfast. But waking up has never been a problem for me living on the farm and having a rooster for an alarm clock. And I'd swear that Bruce probably doesn't get any sleep because he seems to be a night owl.

The archery competition was fun. Floyd Lawton won it. But then something weird happened. This morning, Floyd was gone. Vanished. And no one knows what happened to him. It's almost like he disappeared in the night! Arthur told me he heard of another kid going missing at a previous camp. So that makes two now. I tried to ask the counselors, but they weren't much help. One told me Floyd got sick and left. The other told me that Floyd had a family trip. They can't even get their stories straight!

Is this related to the Scarecrow they keep warning us about? Or is it just some camp story to keep us scared? I've heard others talk about seeing things in the woods at night. Or scratches on their cabin doors. Or maybe we're all just getting spooked over nothing.

TUESDAY – CALL SHEET

6:00 A.M.	-	**Wake Up**
8:00	-	**Cabin Inspection**
8:30	-	**Breakfast**
9:00	-	**Assembly Hall Songs**
10:00	-	**Arts & Crafts**
12:00 P.M.	-	**Lunch**
1:00	-	**Lake** (swimming, boats)
3:00	-	**ACTIVITY #3** (Canoe Race)
5:00	-	**Free Time**
7:00	-	**Dinner**
8:00	-	**Assembly Hall**
9:00	-	**Lights Out**

CAW CAW . . . THE SCARECROW IS OUT THERE

STORAGE CLOSET — INVENTORY REPORT

* ITEMS REMOVED FROM STUDENTS UPON ENTRY TO RETREAT
* NO ELECTRONICS ALLOWED — NO EXCEPTIONS

ITEM #	DESCRIPTION	QTY	NOTES
0008	UTILITY BELT WITH SMOKE BOMBS, FIRECRACKERS, KEYS	1	BELONGS TO BRUCE WAYNE
0009	STORAGE CLOSET BLUEPRINTS	1	CONFISCATED FROM CABIN 2 DURING ROUTINE CHECK
0010	COMPUTER LAPTOP, DIGITAL PAD, FLASH DRIVE	1 EACH	BELONGS TO VIC STONE
0011	PIES	17	FOUND IN CABIN 2 DURING ROUTINE CHECK; RESTOCK AND LOCK KITCHEN

CLARK'S SCRAPBOOK
EVERGREEN ARTS & CRAFTS

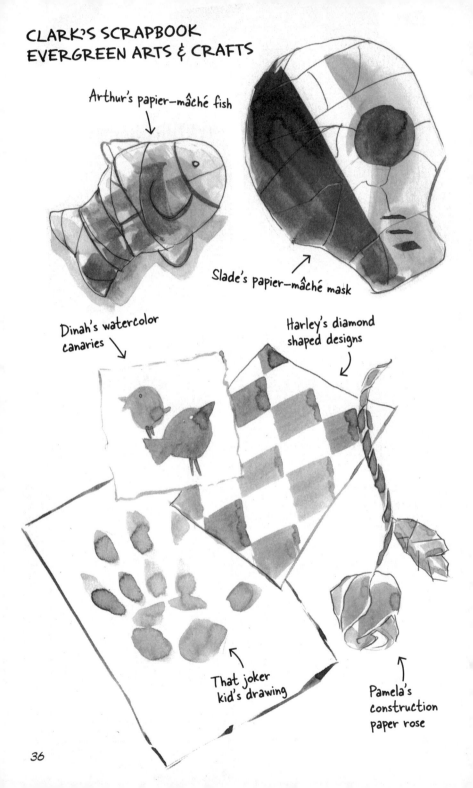

Arthur's papier-mâché fish

Slade's papier-mâché mask

Dinah's watercolor canaries

Harley's diamond shaped designs

That joker kid's drawing

Pamela's construction paper rose

COME SPEND AN AFTERNOON AT THE LAKE ! ! !

- SWIMMING (don't worry . . . no piranhas)
- FISHING (also no piranhas)
- SUNBATHING (piranhas . . . just kidding)
- TIRE SWING (tired of walking, then swing)
- LOG ROLLING (have fun running to nowhere)

CANOES, KAYAKS & BOATS AVAILABLE
(MUST BE CHECKED OUT WITH DEPOSIT)

IF INTERESTED . . .
PLEASE SEE ARTHUR (that's me!)

*** LIFEGUARD ON DUTY ***
12:00 p.m. to 5:00 p.m.

INCIDENT REPORT

STUDENT: Barry Allen

DESCRIPTION OF THE INCIDENT:

Barry was caught passing notes between camps. Also sneaking out at night to put mud inside everyone's shoes.

ACTION TAKEN:

Barry has been given the task of garbage detail around camp and clearing the hiking trails.

ADDITIONAL NOTES:

Barry continues to be a problem. He is exceptionally fast and evasive. We can only imagine the other problems he's causing that we don't know about. He's a potential candidate.

Was able to get a photocopy of this report from the office without being seen. The counselors are really keeping track of all of us. It's got me worried there's something else going on. And what do they mean by candidate?

GATOR LAKE
SAFETY RULES

- Ø **No food or drinking near the lake** (cafeteria only)

- Ø **No horsing around** (or fishing around . . . lake humor)

- Ø **No swimming after dark** (seriously . . . no lights out here)

- Ø **No diving off boats** (that's what diving boards are for)

- Ø **Do not swallow the water** (ew, gross)

- Δ **Leave the water if told to do so** (by Arthur)

IT'S CALLED "GATOR" LAKE FOR A REASON . . .
PLAY IT SAFE

MISSING!
HAVE YOU SEEN ME?
LAST SEEN NEAR THE LAKE

43

 I almost won that race. But even with the lasso, my partner wasn't very willing.

 Don't get me started.

You didn't. You were left at the starting line. HAH!

 Clark, that was funny! Kind of like Bruce sinking in the lake.

Please stop sending me notes.

Lighten up, Bruce. We still love you.

 While you guys are joking, people are going missing.

What do you mean, Bruce?

Dinah's vanished. She never returned to her cabin. She went missing after the canoe race.

Has anyone seen her?

I asked the counselors. They said she had a sore throat.

That shouldn't send her home. Even I know that's a lame excuse!

Who said she went home?

Watch your backs.

CLARK'S JOURNAL

The third day of camp is more of the same. More bad cafeteria food, more pranks, more activities, and more disappearances. Another student has gone missing.

I hate to admit, I might have to start thinking like Bruce. Or at least listening to him.

Pa always said when there are holes in the field . . . start kicking over rocks to find those gophers. It looks like we'll have to kick some rocks.

It's too bad. I was enjoying this camp at first. But now I think it might be safer to come home. But we're not done here yet. And I'm not a quitter.

Hey, Pete,

Evergreen has been an interesting experience. But I look forward to getting back and seeing you and Lana. Maybe we can go to a movie or have a soda at the diner together.

Hope things are going well at home. Check up on my ma and pa when you get the chance. I haven't heard from them since getting here.

By the time you get this letter, I'll probably be done with camp and heading back to Smallville anyways.

- C.K.

WEDNESDAY - CALL SHEET

6:00 A.M. - **Wake Up**

8:00 - **Cabin Inspection**

8:30 - **Breakfast**

9:00 - **Assembly Hall Songs**

10:00 - **Nature Guide**

12:00 P.M. - **Lunch**

2:00 - **Pie-Eating Contest**

4:00 - **ACTIVITY #4** (Hide-and-seek)

5:00 - **Free Time**

7:00 - **Dinner**

8:00 - **Square Dancing**

9:00 - **Lights Out**

DID THE SCARECROW
SCRATCH YOUR CABIN DOOR TONIGHT?

STORAGE CLOSET — INVENTORY REPORT

* ITEMS REMOVED FROM STUDENTS UPON ENTRY TO RETREAT
* NO ELECTRONICS ALLOWED — NO EXCEPTIONS

ITEM #	DESCRIPTION	QTY	NOTES
0012	RUBBER CHICKEN	1	BELONGS TO JOE KERR
0013	YO-YO	1	CONFISCATED FROM HARLEEN QUINZEL; USED TO HIT OTHER STUDENTS
0014	WATER GUN	1	BELONGS TO JOE KERR; APPEARS TO HAVE LEMON JUICE INSIDE
0015	CORK GUN	1	CONFISCATED FROM HARLEEN QUINZEL; ALSO CONTAINS "BANG" FLAG ATTACHMENT
0016	CROWBAR	1	TAKEN FROM TOOL SHED; FOUND DURING ROUTINE CABIN INSPECTION

INCIDENT REPORT

STUDENT: _Barry Allen_

DESCRIPTION OF THE INCIDENT:
Barry was caught starting a water balloon fight. There are discrepancies in the surveillance footage. But it appears that he is able to be everywhere when throwing balloons at students. This suggests multiple Barry Allens, or some other camera trick.

ACTION TAKEN:
Barry has been sent to serve the rest of his time working in the kitchen. He will report there from now on.

ADDITIONAL NOTES:
Our monitoring systems continue to have trouble tracking Barry. Updates pending.

So they are watching us closely! And for what purpose? This seems to be something more than just camp security. Wait until Bruce finds out!

LUNCH MENU

ITEMS AVAILABLE TODAY!

PIZZA DAY
(EVERY DAY)

BBQ BURGERS & SLOPPY JOES
(LOTS O' NAPKINS SO EAT MESSY!)

CHICKEN SANDWICH
(COME BOK FOR SECONDS)

SPAGHETTI & MEATBALLS
(SPA-GET IT WHILE IT'S HOT)

NACHOS GRANDE
(NOT CHO SNACK NO MORE)

EVER GREEN LEAF LETTUCE SALAD BAR
(WITH ALL THE FIXIN'S, EVEN BUGS IF YOU'RE NOT CAREFUL)

CLARK'S JOURNAL

Since the counselors are always around, I decided to approach them during lunch to get to the bottom of things. It didn't go smoothly.

I don't think they're even listening or being honest. They seem uninterested in talking about anything other than the competitions. And they provide very vague answers. When I asked why so many students have gone missing, they seemed surprised like they were hearing it for the first time. That's a lie! When I tried to question them further, they marched me into the kitchen to work.

They're smiling all the time, like they're trying to hide something. It's creepy. Fake and forced. Even Bruce has different facial expressions, which is usually a range between grumpy to annoyed.

There are no camp phones, so we can't call home. And no letters can be sent either. It's kind of like we're trapped here like prisoners.

I've come up with the theory that any students that show exception, including winning, seem to be the ones targeted. Diana agrees with me, and Bruce says my theory seems sound.

I'm going to put it to the test by winning the next competition. That way, I'll see if I disappear. I hope I'm wrong.

PIE-EATING CONTEST

ARE YOU HUNGRY?

BRING YOURSELVES AND YOUR
APPETITE TO THE ASSEMBLY HALL
TODAY AT 2:00 P.M.

WE'LL HAVE APPLE, BLUEBERRY,
PUMPKIN, RHUBARB, AND CHOCOLATE
PIES IN THE COMPETITION. THE
STUDENT WHO EATS THE MOST WILL
BE CROWNED THE PIE KING OR QUEEN!

55

57

MISSING!

HAVE YOU SEEN US?
INFORMATION NEEDED
PLEASE CONTACT CLARK

CLARK'S JOURNAL

What I feared has happened. Another student has gone missing. Right after he won the pie-eating contest, all traces of Barry Allen have disappeared. No one has seen him since he won the crown. All of his personal items are gone. He never reported back to kitchen duty. He's just vanished.

And it's my fault.

Bruce says it was a good thing that I lost the pie-eating contest. Otherwise I'd be the one missing. But that was my intent. It might've been my only way to find out where the missing students have gone. Barry's gone because of me (and his speed . . . man, that kid is fast)!

The counselors have given up trying to provide excuses. This time they claim even they don't know where Barry is. That he has a history for practical jokes and is probably pulling this one himself. In any other circumstance, I'd be inclined to agree. But not this time.

61

"EVER STRANGE"

by *Daily Planet* Junior Reporter, Lois Lane

During my week spent at Evergreen Adventure Retreat in the mountains, I found many secrets hidden from the public. Some concerned monsters in the forest and lake, passed off as scary stories by camp students. Lights in the night sky could be a UFO. Even students who exhibited special abilities would go missing, never to be seen again. As I tried to dig deeper to see what I could find, I was blocked from access or help. Eventually the counselors lost interest in me so they sent me home early back to Metropolis, whether they were annoyed or just wanted to shut me up. But now I have the chance to tell my side of the story.

(Continued on page Z-22)

I followed the lights into the woods. Sounds and lights. They didn't want to be seen or heard. But I saw and I heard. Who are they? Why are they here? I tried to get close, but something kept me away. Was it fear? Or some invisible barrier between us? Had I tipped them off to my presence? The wind shifted in the trees. First I was looking for them. Now they were looking for me. I ran as fast as I could, trying not to leave a trail. But they continue to track me. Continue to hound my every step. I will record my memories in full detail in my conspiracy blog, Sage Advice. Until then, I remain . . .

Sage Advice

**GRAB YOUR PARTNER
AND DO-SI-DO TO A NIGHT OF . . .**

SQUARE DANCING

8:00 p.m. IN THE ASSEMBLY HALL

MUSIC BY **DJ VIBE**

REFRESHMENTS WILL BE PROVIDED

ATTENDANCE MANDATORY!

CLARK'S JOURNAL

Now Pam is missing. More and more students at camp are disappearing. There's more empty seats in the cafeteria. More cabins that have empty bunks. It's getting out of control. It's making everyone paranoid, not just Bruce.

The only ones who aren't alarmed are the counselors. What is their problem? They should be just as worried as us that they're losing campers!

From what I saw in the fort, it's been happening to other groups of students even before us. If the counselors won't help us, then we need to find help wherever we can!

Bruce's plan involves Diana distracting the counselors, while he breaks into their office and we use their computer to send out emails. I can't believe I'm going along with this, but it seems like we have to try . . .

DEAR LOIS,

I READ YOUR ARTICLE ABOUT EVERGREEN. I'M ACTUALLY A
STUDENT HERE AT THE ADVENTURE CAMP. AND STRANGE THINGS
KEEP GOING ON. STUDENTS ARE DISAPPEARING. AND I'M
WORRIED MY FRIENDS OR I MIGHT BE NEXT. I HOPE THIS
REACHES YOU THAT YOU MIGHT BE ABLE TO HELP SHED
FURTHER LIGHT ON THIS RETREAT AND SEND HELP. THANKS.

— CLARK

TO: GCPD
RE: CRIMINAL ACTIVITY

I WOULD LIKE TO FILE A COMPLAINT AGAINST THE EVERGREEN
ADVENTURE CAMP. STUDENTS ARE GOING MISSING AND I THINK
THE STAFF IS RESPONSIBLE. SEND THE SPECIAL CRIMES
UNIT TO THIS ADDRESS AND THE K-9 UNIT TO SNIFF THINGS
OUT. MAKE SURE MY REQUEST IS GIVEN PRIORITY AND IS
BROUGHT TO THE ATTENTION OF DETECTIVE JAMES GORDON.
HE SEEMS LIKE SOMEONE THAT WILL HELP GET THE JOB DONE.

SINCERELY,

BRUCE WAYNE

< ERROR >

< DELIVERY TO THE FOLLOWING RECIPIENTS
FAILED PERMANENTLY >

< ADDRESSES NOT RECOGNIZED ON SERVER >

< REJECTED FOR THE RECIPIENT DOMAIN >

THURSDAY - CALL SHEET

6:00 A.M.	-	**Wake Up**
8:00	-	**Cabin Inspection**
8:30	-	**Breakfast**
9:00	-	**Assembly Hall Songs**
10:00	-	**Free Time**
12:00 P.M.	-	**Lunch**
1:00	-	**Survival Guide**
3:00	-	**ACTIVITY #5** (Obstacle Course)
5:00	-	**Free Time**
7:00	-	**Dinner**
8:00	-	**Talent Show**
9:00	-	**Lights Out**

DON'T BE AFRAID OF THE DARK,
BE AFRAID OF THE SCARECROW!

72

CRIME INVESTIGATION UNIT - POSSIBLE MEMBERS

Δ   VIC STONE = Whiz with computers and technology

?   OLLIE QUEEN = Sharpshooter with an arrow and wit;
      huge ego can be a problem

Δ   ARTHUR CURRY = Likable all-around good guy

Δ   ZATANNA = Magic tricks could be useful; speaks
      backward a lot

?   MARI = Don't know much about her; animal lover

      LENNY SNART = Angry and distant

      SLADE WILSON = Doesn't like Vic

?   SELINA KYLE = Not sure if trustworthy

      CIRCE = Bad magic

      PRISCILLA RICH = Snobby, harsh, savage

?   HARLEEN QUINZEL = Hard to tell, obnoxious, but can
      have a sweet side

      LOUISE LINCOLN = Like Lenny, has a cold disposition

Hey, Vic! We haven't had a chance to talk much, but you seem pretty cool.

 Thanks, Clark! Means a lot.

 It's weird, you know. Everyone going missing.

 I know. Something's not right. Even their "no electronics or technology" policy.

 Would you like to do something about it?

 I'm listening.

 There's a group of us that are investigating. We need more students willing to help.

 I'm down with that. Only problem is, they've got all my stuff locked up in storage.

 I'd really be able to do some damage once I get my computers and equipment back.

 Bruce has the same thoughts. You two should get together.

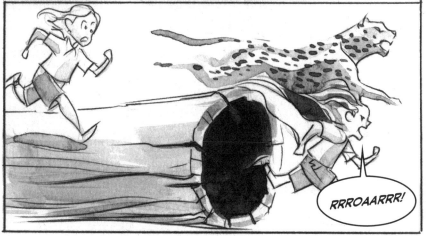

CLARK'S SCRAPBOOK - NOTES

 Diana, I need you to keep an eye on Mari.

 Now that she's won the competition, she'll be the next one to go missing.

 Will do, Clark. Plus it gives me a chance to enlist her in our investigation.

 What about Bruce?

 Bruce and I along with Vic are going to try to break into the storage room to get their stuff back.

Plus there's no idea what else we might find in there.

When are you planning this?

During the talent show.

It'll provide the perfect distraction with everyone there.

Good luck!

You too.

Mari has a special connection to nature and the animal spirits that guide her and grant her their powers.

Mari helped me make this chart so anyone can figure out theirs. To find out what your animal spirit guide is, just take the first letter in your first name. And that is your animal spirit.

ANIMAL SPIRIT GUIDE CHART

A = Aardvark

B = Bat

C = Lion

D = Dove

E = Elephant

F = Monkey

G = Hippo

H = Tiger

I = Fox

J = Snake

K = Crocodile

L = Gazelle

M = Porcupine

N = Panther

O = Rhino

P = Cheetah

Q = Kangaroo

R = Lizard

S = Bear

T = Turtle

U = Walrus

V = Vulture

W = Eagle

X = Phoenix

Y = Wolf

Z = Rabbit

84

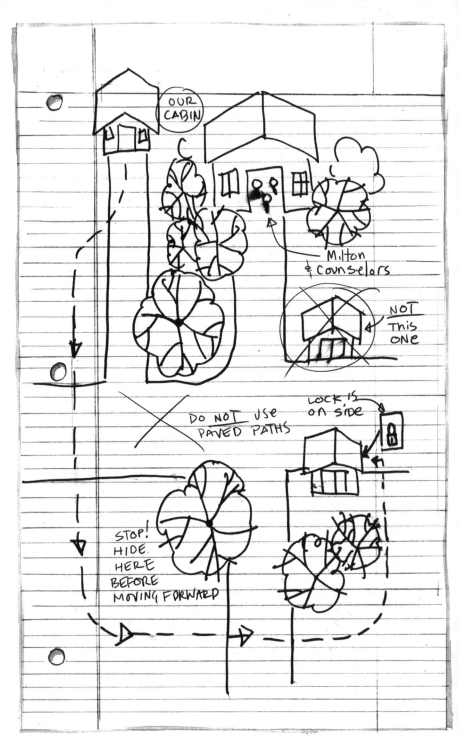

OPERATION: STORAGE WAR

DO operate quickly and quietly.

DO have a lookout.

DON'T yell "LOOK OUT" and attract attention.

DO open the door using lock-picking tools.

DON'T use your fists or feet or head.

DON'T use your secret heat vision.

DO use stealth by hiding in shadows.

DON'T get scared of your own shadow.

DON'T set off the alarm.

DON'T get caught.

DO get your stuff back.

DON'T get locked inside.

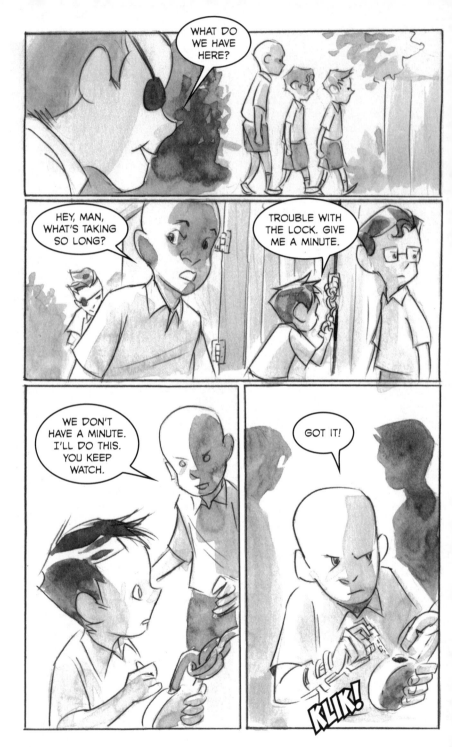

LIGHTS, CAMERA, ACTION!
COME SHOW US WHAT YOU'RE MADE OF . . .

EVERGREEN TALENT SHOW

ASSEMBLY HALL 8:00 p.m.

PEFORM ON STAGE
NO ACT TURNED AWAY
PARTICIPATION MANDATORY

GOT TALENT?

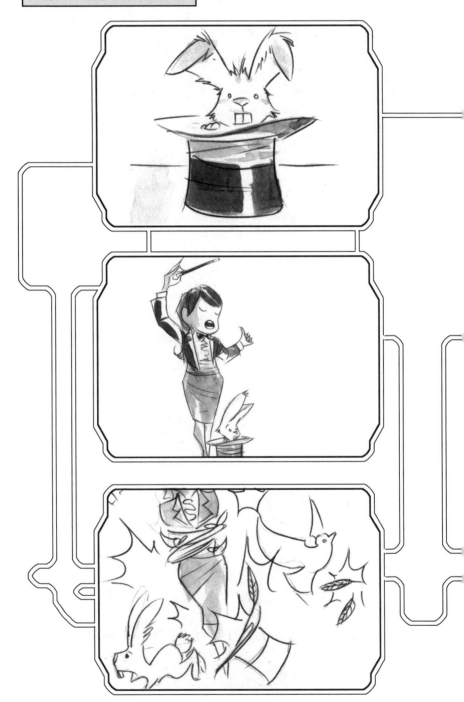

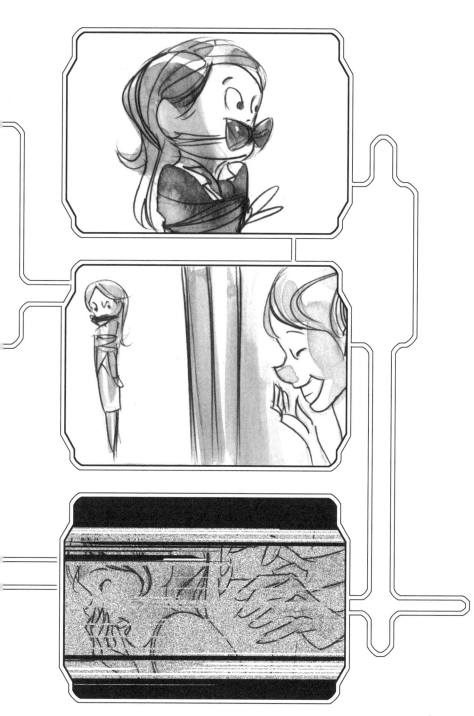

93

While we were breaking into the storage closet, the talent show took place. I was able to get copies of the score cards. It's confusing to read the counselors' thoughts on each performance. They're not grading them on their talents as much as what they're looking for, which is very unsettling.

NAME:	JOE KERR
SCORE:	12 (DEDUCTIONS FOR SQUIRTING LEMON JUICE AT THE AUDIENCE AND BAD PUNS)
NOTES:	THIS JOKER TELLS AWFUL JOKES AND NONSENSE. CHAOTIC AND UNPREDICTABLE. NOT THE "TALENT" WE ARE INTERESTED IN.

NAME:	OLIVER QUEEN
SCORE:	**74** (DEDUCTIONS FOR ARROGANCE; BUT POINTS FOR SKILL)
NOTES:	OLLIE HAS PROVEN GREAT MARKSMANSHIP BEING ABLE TO HIT TARGETS. ACQUIRING HIS SKILLS CAN UPGRADE OUR OWN TARGETING SYSTEM.

NAME:	LOUISE LINCOLN
SCORE:	80
NOTES:	LOUISE IS ABLE TO GENERATE FROZEN ICE AND MOLD IT INTO ANY FORM. SHE CAN CREATE A COLD WIND, FREEZE THE GROUND, OR CREATE ICE SCULPTURES AS PART OF HER SKILLS. HER "TALENT" CAN BE ADDED TO OUR OWN.

NAME:	PRISCILLA RICH
SCORE:	UNDETERMINED
NOTES:	SHE HAS EXHIBITED INCREASED PHYSICAL ATTRIBUTES BUT HAS PRESENTED NONE OF THOSE SKILLS HERE. HER MUSICAL APTITUDE IS ADEQUATE BUT UNNEEDED.

NAME:	SELINA KYLE
SCORE:	UNDETERMINED
NOTES:	MUCH LIKE PRISCILLA, SELINA HAS ACROBATIC SKILL AND AN AFFINITY FOR GUILE AND STEALTH. BUT ALSO IS VERY INDEPENDENT. UNSURE HOW TO PROCEED.

CLARK'S JOURNAL

We got our stuff back from the locked storage closet. Cool! But they totally lied to us about the phones. And it looked like they destroyed them on purpose. Who does that? And what else are they lying to us about? I can't believe this camp is still in business!

No one is coming to help us, so we'll help ourselves. And we already have a plan.

It used to be just Diana, Bruce, and me. But we invited Vic to help out. And with all his computer stuff back, he thinks he'll be able to get online and contact others. And we've got more friends here at camp who we're going to recruit. There's safety in numbers. And if we're all working together, we'll be able to find the missing students, I just know it!

We lost Mari though. Diana has taken it the hardest. But I told her it's not her fault. We'll find who's responsible and make them pay. Trust me, I wouldn't want to get on Diana's bad side!

FRIDAY - CALL SHEET

FREE DAY

6:00 A.M.	-	**Wake Up**
8:00	-	**Cabin Inspection**
8:30	-	**Breakfast**
12:00 P.M.	-	**Lunch**
7:00	-	**Dinner**
9:00	-	**Lights Out**

THE ONLY THING TO FEAR IS . . .
THE SCARECROW!

Since we have the whole day to
ourselves, it's time to take action.
Gather the troops and storm the
compound. Gather intel. Seize the day!

ATTENTION,

REMAINING STUDENTS ! ! !

THERE IS A CONSPIRACY TO COVER UP

THE DISAPPEARANCE OF STUDENTS AT

EVERGREEN. IF YOU ARE INTERESTED

IN GETTING TO THE TRUTH, KEEP YOUR

EYES PEELED. WE WILL MEET AT THE

LAKE TODAY TO TALK MORE ABOUT IT.

TELL NO ONE

 **SUGGESTION BOX**

DO YOU HAVE A QUESTION OR CONCERN FOR THE
STAFF? PLEASE WRITE IT BELOW AND WE WILL SUPPLY
AN ANSWER.

YOUR CONCERN:

Students are missing. And no one on staff
seems worried. You provide no answers and
don't care. You aren't even mailing any of our
letters. What do you say to that?

STAFF RESPONSE:

NO ONE IS MISSING. EVERYONE IS PRESENT AND
ACCOUNTED FOR. THANK YOU FOR YOUR INQUIRY.
HAVE A NICE DAY.

The counselors have
a suggestion box for
students to write
down any questions or
concerns for the staff
to answer. I filled out
one to see if it would
be read. This is their
troubling response.

Thought I'd put the camera I found in the fort to use. Try to document what the director and counselors do.

Smiling. Always smiling.

What is he doing here?

Probably up to no good.

Have you noticed how quiet it is? Milton and the counselors haven't been around.

Good! Their smiles were annoying me.

 How's about my smile?

Slightly less annoying.

I passed out all the fliers to the cabins. We're meeting at the lake to plan what to do next.

 Hey, everyone! It's Vic. Thanks for helping me get back my computer equipment from storage.

I've hooked up your phones with encryption, purged any bugs, and installed protection from any hidden viruses.

 We can text again!

I'm beginning to like this guy.

we're back online!

 aww . . . i'm going to miss writing and passing notes. was kind of fun.

 if you like carpal tunnel syndrome

 lol

< SOMEONE NEW HAS ENTERED THE ROOM >

 you all started without me

 VIC!!

 hey, everyone!

thanks for hooking us back up with our phones.

this will make things easier now.

 no prob

SEND

how is your computer doing?

 it's going through a system reboot. i want to make sure they didn't do anything to it while it's been locked up.

good idea

time to meet at the lake and gather our forces

 ROLL OUT! if we had wheels . . . which would be cool.

SEND

CLARK'S JOURNAL

The "Creature in the Lake" mystery has been solved. It wasn't some monster or croc, but just some scared kid. Glad at least one of us has come back from being missing. Waylon's return has given us all hope. The others might still be out there somewhere. We just need to go find them.

Maybe solving some of the other mysteries will get us closer to that happening? And I should go back to the fort. I need to see what evidence I can gather there so we can get started.

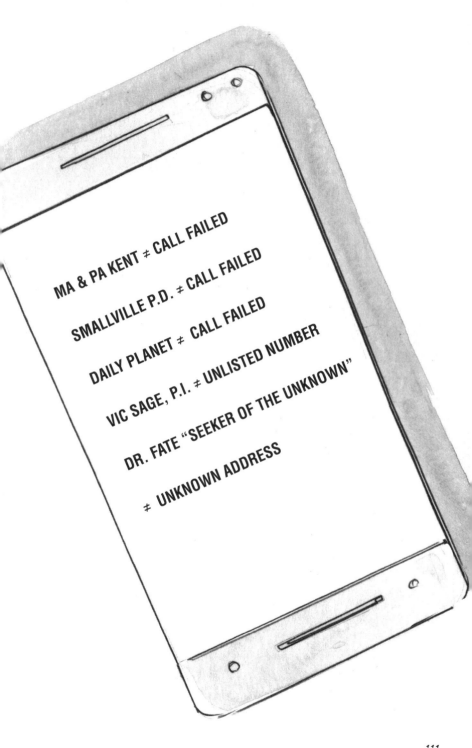

MA & PA KENT ≠ CALL FAILED

SMALLVILLE P.D. ≠ CALL FAILED

DAILY PLANET ≠ CALL FAILED

VIC SAGE, P.I. ≠ UNLISTED NUMBER

DR. FATE "SEEKER OF THE UNKNOWN"

≠ UNKNOWN ADDRESS

there might be some truth to them.

they're just stories to scare kids

ok let's prove it.

are you sure this is a good use of our time?

if it helps us get closer to finding the missing kids, then it's worth it.

agreed then. what should we do?

i'll get Vic and we'll go look for the bigfoot.

you and Bruce get to the bottom of that bogeyman scaring students.

already solved. it's batman!

i am kinda scary.

LOL

go ahead and wear your "uniforms" if it makes you feel any better.

SEND

119

CLARK'S JOURNAL

We've solved two more monster mysteries. I think we're on a roll!

The "bogeyman" turned out to be Jonathan Crane. A scrawny kid who came to this camp previously. The other students picked on him and to get back at them, he decided to dress up as a scarecrow. It was something that always scared him and now he could scare others. He stuck around because he enjoyed it. But he's not responsible for the missing students. But he gave us a tip who is . . . and it's someone not human. Now I'm the one that's a little scared!

If it's not human, then maybe the animal that Vic and I found could be responsible. But that "Bigfoot" turned out to be a gorilla named Grodd. When Vic searched on his computer, he found that Grodd had recently escaped from the zoo. And the timeline doesn't match up with the other missing students from before we came to camp. Once we find the missing students, maybe we can help get Grodd back to the zoo.

SATURDAY - CALL SHEET

6:00 A.M. - **Wake Up**

8:00 - **Cabin Inspection**

8:30 - **Breakfast**

9:00 - **Assembly Hall Songs**

10:00 - **Arts & Crafts**

12:00 P.M. - **Lunch**

1:00 - **Capture the Flag**

3:00 - **ACTIVITY #6** (Tug-o'-war)

5:00 - **Free Time**

7:00 - **Dinner**

9:00 - **Lights Out**

CLARK'S SCRAPBOOK
ARTS & CRAFTS

Bruce

Selina

Oliver

100 50 25 5

Arthur

That Joker kid

Barry

Capture the Flag

Sign up

CANCELED
DUE TO LACK OF AVAILABLE PLAYERS.

125

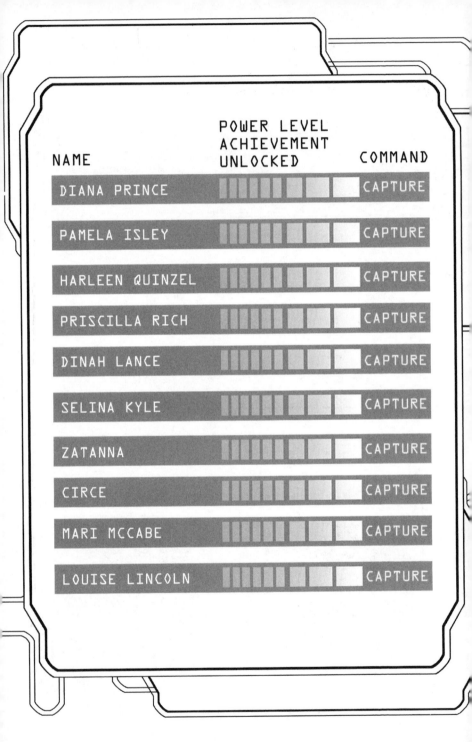

NAME	POWER LEVEL ACHIEVEMENT UNLOCKED		COMMAND
DIANA PRINCE			CAPTURE
PAMELA ISLEY			CAPTURE
HARLEEN QUINZEL			CAPTURE
PRISCILLA RICH			CAPTURE
DINAH LANCE			CAPTURE
SELINA KYLE			CAPTURE
ZATANNA			CAPTURE
CIRCE			CAPTURE
MARI MCCABE			CAPTURE
LOUISE LINCOLN			CAPTURE

NAME	POWER LEVEL ACHIEVEMENT UNLOCKED	COMMAND
CLARK KENT		CAPTURE
ARTHUR CURRY		CAPTURE
BRUCE WAYNE		CAPTURE
JOE KERR		CAPTURE
BARRY ALLEN		CAPTURE
LENNY SNART		CAPTURE
VIC STONE		CAPTURE
SLADE WILSON		CAPTURE
OLIVER QUEEN		CAPTURE
FLOYD LAWTON		CAPTURE

131

133

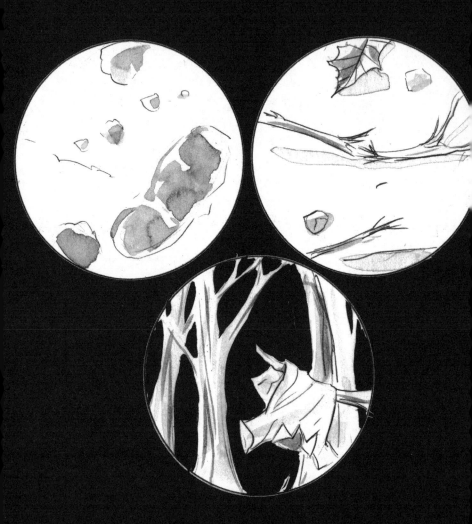

vic, you there?

what do ya need, CK?

can you interrupt the androids' tracking systems?

maybe send them a cyber virus.

even better. i'll send them them a cyborg virus.

< UPLOAD SENDING . . . >

< UPLOAD COMPLETE >

SEND

<SYSTEM ERROR>

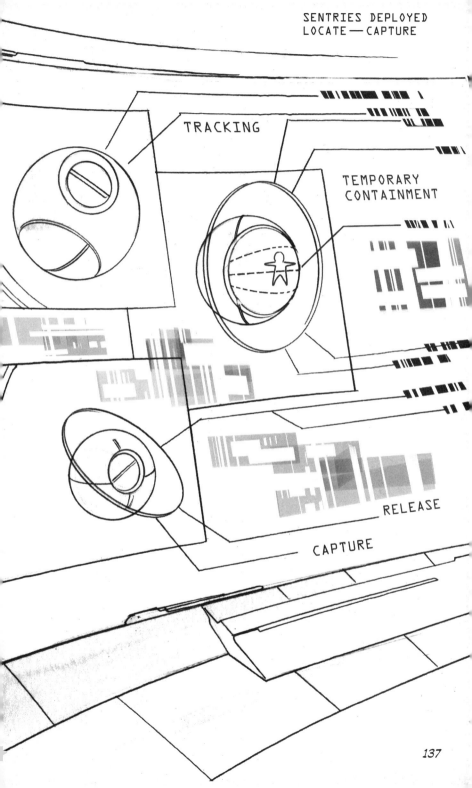

<TARGET ACQUIRED>
<PRINCE, DIANA>
<LASSO IN STORAGE>

<TARGET ACQUIRED>
<STONE, VIC>
<SLEEP MODE ACTIVATED — OVERRIDE DENIED>

<TARGETS ACQUIRED>
<SNART, LENNY>
<LINCOLN, LOUISE>
〖 REPAIRING FROZEN FILES 〗

<TARGETS SEARCHING . . . >
〖 SYSTEM SHUTDOWN TO REPAIR ACIDIC DAMAGE 〗

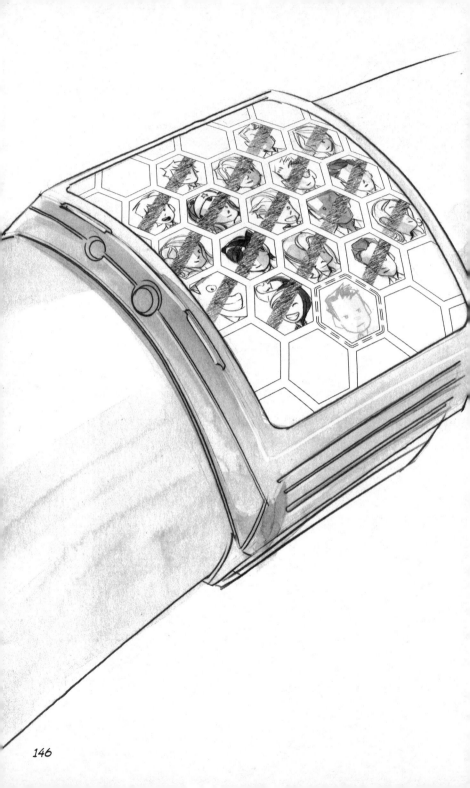

149

bruce, are you there?

tell me you found some way to escape!

bruce!

diana!

are you there, vic? found a way to reactivate yourself?

someone?

anyone??

?

SEND

<I FIRST TRIED TO STUDY ALL OF YOU AT SCHOOL>
<BUT TIME WAS CUT SHORT DUE TO EARLY TERMINATION>
<I PLANNED TO STUDY YOU AT EVERGREEN>
<UNHINDERED>
<UNINTERRUPTED>
<TO PUSH YOU, TEST YOU, STUDY YOUR POWERS>
<AND WHEN THEY WERE AT THEIR PEAK — TO REPLICATE THEM>
<TO MERGE ALL INTO ONE CONSTRUCT>
<TO TAKE OVER THE WORLD>

156

IT IS USELESS TO RESIST

YOU ARE THE FINAL PIECE

YOU WILL MAKE A GREAT
FINAL ADDITION TO
DOWNLOAD

AND THEN TO DISPLAY

ACCESSING BRAINWAVE
PATTERNS TO REPROGRAM

ACCESSING . . .

160

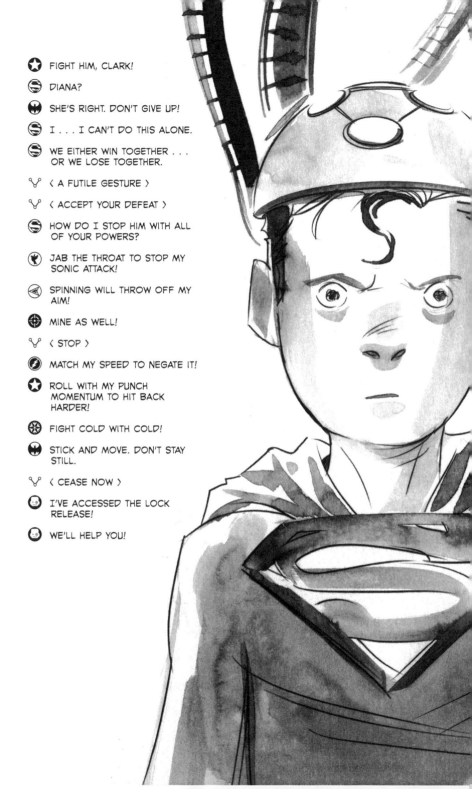

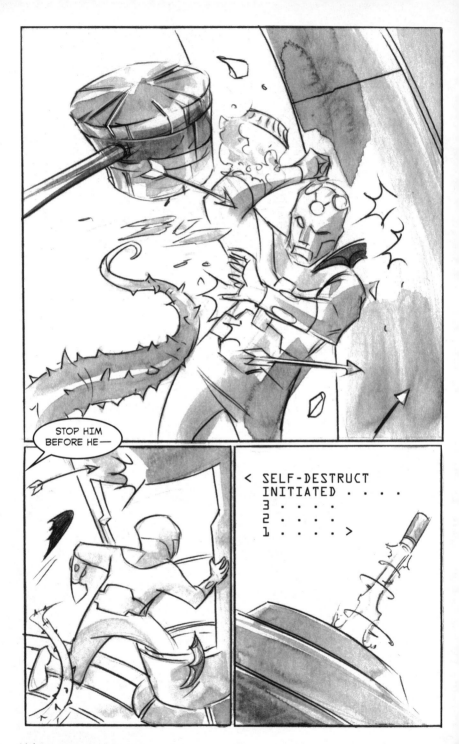

i've got the satellite uplink confirmed.

and search for brainiac still pending.

any data you have, send it over

i'd like to try to search for brainiac with my computer.

what type do you have?

. . . a pretty nice one

heh ok.

uploading files to your server account.

< DATA RECEIVED >

so when do I get to see your computer, bruce?

< USER HAS LOGGED OFF >

that guy has a better vanishing act than zatanna!

SEND

```
ACCESS PORT = BATCAVE
ROOM = PRIVATE
USERS = ACTIVE (2)
```

 INPUT DATA DUMP INTO BATCOMPUTER TO TRACK POD

I'M A BUTLER, NOT A HACKER, SIR

ALFRED!

I'M AFRAID THE COMPUTER IS UNABLE TO LOCATE IT

KEEP TRYING

I ALWAYS DO

I'VE TRACKED YOUR WHEREABOUTS AS WELL, MASTER BRUCE

I'M SURPRISED YOU'RE STILL AT CAMP

I CONCLUDE YOU ENJOYED YOURSELF?

I GUESS I DID

SPLENDID

AND DID YOU RECEIVE THE
PUDDING CUPS I SENT?

ALFRED, I'M KIND OF BUSY
RIGHT NOW.

I HOPE THAT A WEEK IN THE
WOODS DID NOT LEAD TO A WEEK
WITHOUT A BATH . . .

ALFRED, I'M BUSY!!!!!

169

170

171

CLARK'S JOURNAL

Evergreen Adventure Camp really was an adventure! The mountains were beautiful to see. I loved hiking in the forest. I took all sorts of nature photos to add to my scrapbook. They still can't make me lick a banana slug though. And the lake was refreshing. Diana was able to push Bruce into the water even without my help. Hey . . . someone had to take the photo of it happening!

Most of all, it was fun hanging out with friends and making new ones. Better yet, we united together to stop Brainiac. Who knew that our old school library computer would end up really being an evil android? Still it would be nice to get together and not have to fight robots or ninjas or other bad things. But this hero thing doesn't look like it's going away, and with more enemies out there just looking to make trouble, it's nice to have more of us around to help when we can.

So I know you're wondering about our new team name. So am I! Barry said he's going to give it some "serious thought." But he's a prankster, so anything can happen. But I'm sure we'll find something that works for just us. Hmmmm . . .

The sooner we're a team, the sooner we can go out there and save the world. I can't even imagine who we'll have to go up against next.

174

Derek Fridolfs

Derek Fridolfs works in the comic industry as a writer, artist, and inker on many beloved properties. With Dustin Nguyen, he co-wrote the Eisner-nominated *Batman: Li'l Gotham*. He's also written and worked on such titles as *Batman: Arkham City Endgame*, *Arkham Unhinged*, *Detective Comics*, *Legends of the Dark Knight*, *Adventures of Superman*, *Sensation Comics Featuring Wonder Woman*, *Catwoman*, *Zatanna*, *JLA*, *Justice League Beyond*, and comics based on the cartoons for *Adventure Time*, *Regular Show*, *Clarence*, *Pig Goat Banana Cricket*, *Dexter's Laboratory*, *Teenage Mutant Ninja Turtles*, *Teen Titans Go*, *Looney Tunes*, and *Scooby-Doo Where Are You!* This is his second children's book.

Dustin Nguyen

Dustin Nguyen is a *New York Times* bestselling and Eisner Award–winning American comics creator. His body of work includes the co-creation of *Batman: Li'l Gotham*, numerous DC, Marvel, Dark Horse, and Boom! titles along with Image Comics' *Descender*, which he co-created. He lives in California with his wife, Nicole; their two kids, Bradley and Kaeli; and dog, Max. His first children's picture book, titled *What Is It?*, is written by his wife (at the age of 10) and is their first collaboration together. He enjoys sleeping and driving.